Lucy's Family Tree

KAREN HALVORSEN SCHRECK *Illustrated by* STEPHEN GASSLER III

TILBURY HOUSE  PUBLISHERS

GARDINER, MAINE

"I'm different," Lucy said one day after school.

Dad looked up from the photograph he was framing, one that he had taken. He didn't take pictures like other people. His were beautiful, yes, but they were blurry and big, too. His were different.

"Today Ms. Magritte told us we had to make a family tree," Lucy said. Everyone in the whole class has to do it. But Marco teased me on the bus and said I couldn't make a tree. He said I was different." Lucy blinked back tears. "Marco's right. I'm weird."

"No," Dad said. "You are *not* weird."

Dad put down the photograph and held out his hand. After a moment, Lucy took hold of it. His grip was firm and familiar.

"You are *different*," Dad said. "But so is everyone in his or her own way. That's not something to be ashamed of, Lucy."

Lucy shook her head fiercely. "Everyone's not different."

"Who's the same?"

"Marco's the same. He was born in Mexico, like me, but his whole family was, too. They're all the same. They look like families are supposed to."

"And how are families supposed to look?"

"The same!" Lucy said loudly, not shouting exactly. "Like on TV, in commercials. With real moms and dads and kids, not adopted ones." And then she pulled her hand from her father's, and ran to her room.

Lucy stared at the photograph on her dresser, one of her family camping last summer. Some other camper had taken it, so it was the right size and in focus. Lucy's dog Perro was the only one who looked like he belonged in her family. People didn't look twice at Perro. People didn't ask questions; they didn't say he was different.

On the floor beside Lucy's dresser was a carved wooden chest from Mexico. Sometimes Lucy opened that chest a lot, and spent hours looking at the things inside; other times she hardly remembered it was there. Other times still, she wished the chest wasn't in her room at all. Once she hid the chest in her closet, only to pull it out a few days later.

Lucy opened the chest now. Inside was a photo album with pictures of the foster family she lived with until she was three months old and Mom and Dad could come and get her. There were also other important things from that time—baby things—and the souvenirs Mom and Dad bought for her while they were in Mexico, for when she was older.

One by one, Lucy carefully lifted these things from the chest. Last of all, she took out her Tree of Life. Trees of Life were a Mexican art form, her parents had said, made of clay and fragile. Lucy held her Tree of Life close. It scared her, how easily it might break.

There was a knock at Lucy's door—Dad's *rat-a-tat-tat.* A moment passed, and then he slowly opened the door. Mom was there, too, wearing one of the dresses she'd sewed. She didn't dress quite like other mothers. The dresses she made were, well, different.

Mom and Dad looked concerned. Lucy saw it in their eyes. And their eyes were warm with something else, too. Love, Lucy thought. When hard stuff came up—school stuff like grades, fickle friends, and boys; family stuff like rules, respect, and adoption—Lucy's parents looked at her with concern and love. With anger, too, sometimes, and sometimes with confusion.

Sometimes? All the time, more like. Hard stuff was coming up a lot these days. Usually the hard stuff led to conversations like these, conversations Lucy didn't necessarily want to have—at least, not at first.

"Lucy." Mom's voice was quiet and calm—the voice Mom used when Lucy needed reassuring. "You *can* make a family tree. A *real* family tree. The one you need to make."

Lucy stared at the floor.

"How do you think it should look?" Dad asked. "What do you think it should be?"

Lucy's head felt as empty as a hole in the ground. She closed her eyes, but nothing would take root in her mind; no ideas would grow.

"Is your assignment due tomorrow?" Dad asked.

"No," Lucy mumbled. "Not for a week."

"Good," Mom said. "We have some time then."

But to Lucy, a week seemed like nothing at all. No time is long enough to finish the impossible.

The next night Mom called Lucy to the kitchen. Art supplies lay on the table, and Dad was making watermelon lemonade.

"Sustenance for the journey," he said, setting a full glass on the counter.

Lucy took the glass. She loved watermelon lemonade. "What journey?"

Mom patted a big blank sheet of paper. "Your family tree, of course."

Lucy put the glass down on the table. Obviously she had not made herself clear. "I cannot make a family tree," she said firmly.

"Lucy." Dad's voice was deep. "You have an assignment. We'll talk about it with you, explore some options. Or else you can plunge in on your own, write about it for a bit, maybe sketch a few possibilities."

"No." Lucy was almost shouting. The room felt too small, like Mom and Dad, the art supplies, and walls were closing in. "I'm different. You can write me an excuse."

"Excuses are for being sick and for obstacles you can't overcome." Mom drew herself up tall. "We'll talk about this again on Saturday. Today's Tuesday. That gives you three days to do an assignment for *us*. We want you to make a list of three families who are the same. Think carefully. If you can come up with three that we all agree on, then we'll reconsider your family tree."

"You'll write me an excuse," Lucy said.

"No," Dad said. "We'll do anything we can to help you finish the assignment *your* way." He smiled. "Listen, Lucy. I'll make you a bet. If you're right—if you can find three families who are the same—I'll help you with that flower bed you've been wanting. We'll plant tulips and daffodil bulbs now, and you'll have flowers first thing in the spring."

Lucy thought for a moment, then nodded confidently. "You've got a deal."

Lucy spent most of the next school day thinking about the fact that, for the first time in her life, she knew her parents were really and truly wrong. Loving, yes. Concerned and supportive. But wrong. Because no matter what her parents believed, she *was* different from your ordinary, everyday different. She was truly, truly different. They needed to understand that.

That night, Lucy pulled out a piece of paper. Across the top, she wrote: TYPICAL FAMILIES. She tapped her pencil thoughtfully against her chin, then began to make a list of the people she wanted to think about first, the people she liked. She assumed that if she liked them, they must have something in common. They must be the same.

Soon she had a list of six names. Three of the names were her friends. Three of the names were her parents' friends, the ones she liked best, the ones who were her friends, too.

She knew she would have to study their families carefully, to make sure her parents couldn't find any holes in her argument. She'd heard that phrase on a television show about a lawyer. Lucy thought she might be a lawyer someday. She would think of this assignment as her first case.

The next day at recess, Lucy went to play on the junglegym with her best friend, Lucinda Knapp. Lucy and Lucinda had been best friends for almost a year, ever since the day they learned each other's names, and realized they were almost the same, but weren't. Lucinda had just moved to town, and Lucy had seen her standing alone in the corner of the classroom, nervously twisting the neck of her lunch bag. Lucy couldn't bear to see people who looked lonely. And this lonely person looked like a girl in a magazine. Lucy sometimes (not so much anymore, but sometimes still) wished she looked like that—like a typical American girl. She asked Lucinda to eat lunch with her.

They sat at Lucy's desk, and pretty soon they were laughing hard. They'd laughed like that ever since, usually at jokes other kids thought were dumb. Even now, Lucinda was telling Lucy that kind of a joke.

"Where does the king keep his armies?"

"Where?"

"Up his sleevies!"

Lucy barely heard the joke. She forced a giggle.

Lucinda swung forward on the bar and hung upside down from her knees. Lucy stayed still, the better to direct her questions. Lucinda was Lucy's first case study.

"Lucinda," Lucy said. "You're from a typical family, aren't you? An average American family. The kind everyone wants to be."

Lucinda swung fiercely and penny-dropped to the ground. "How can you say that? You know."

And that's when Lucy remembered. Lucinda's family moved to town because Lucinda's father lost his job. They had to move so Lucinda's mom could find work—and her mom had found work, a really good job. Lucinda's dad kept looking. Then last month, Lucinda's parents said that their family was going to change. Lucinda's dad was going to stay home full time, raising Lucinda and her four younger siblings, and Lucinda's mom was going to be the breadwinner.

"*She's* going to bring home the bacon," Lucinda had whispered to Lucy. "*He's* going to fry it up in a pan. That's what they said! It's an old song or something. I don't even

know it!" It was as if Lucinda was saying, "I don't even know my family." But then she never said another word about the change.

Lucy jumped to the ground. "I thought it was okay now. It's not so bad, is it? Your family's pretty typical, except for that one thing."

"I'm getting used to it, I guess." Lucinda kicked at the dirt. "And my parents seem happier." Then Lucinda looked at Lucy, eyes blazing. "But it's not typical. And I still don't want anyone else to know." She spun around and ran toward the school.

"Your family's cool," Lucy shouted after her. Lucinda didn't turn back.

Lucy stared at Lucinda's footprints, her eyes wide with surprise. Cool was, well, *cool*, but typical was what Lucy wanted—what Lucinda wanted, too, it seemed.

At least Lucy still had five more chances to find three families who weren't different for different reasons.

Lucy knew where to find Robert during study hall: in the library, poring over books on airplanes. Flying was Robert's obsession.

"Hi, Lindbergh," Lucy said.

Robert looked up. "I'll take that as a compliment."

"I have a question for you," Lucy said.

"I'm busy."

"It'll just take a minute."

Robert studied the clock above the librarian's desk. Just before the second hand hit twelve, he said, "Ready and counting."

Lucy laughed.

"That cost you three seconds," Robert said.

"Fine," Lucy said. "You have fifty-two, no, fifty-one seconds to say why you're from a typical family."

"Typical?" Robert watched the second hand. "Not really. I sort of have two moms. There's my biological mom, and then there's Nancy, who has lived with us since I was two. She loves us both, and that makes us a family. Is that the answer you wanted?"

Lucy had seen Robert with two women at one of his soccer games. The women were talking and drinking steaming cups of cider with some of the other parents. When Robert ran up to them, one of the women had hugged him, while the other presented him with a chocolate bar.

"Your time is up," Robert said. "See me later if you want to talk more."

Lucy sat down at another table and tried to read. She couldn't stop twisting her hair around her finger. Whenever she did that, Mom asked her what was wrong. She was glad Mom wasn't around now.

Lucy barely said hello to Mom after school. She ran into the kitchen, stating, "I'm going next door."

Mom looked up, startled. She was holding a Priority Mail envelope in her hands. Usually, Lucy would have asked what was inside, but today, she dashed out the door and through the gap in the hedge to Benjamin's backyard, where the giant oak tree stood. Through the tangle of branches and leaves, she saw the floor of Benjamin's treehouse, heard the strum of a guitar. That would be Benjamin's older sister, Natalie, playing and singing. Natalie was a freshman in high school, and, already, she'd played her guitar in the all-school talent contest and won second place. She'd dedicated the winning song, her own composition, to her family.

Natalie was playing the last chords of that song now.

As the final notes faded away, Lucy rang the bell that hung from the lowest tree branch. There was a rustle in the leaves above, and a ladder came clattering down. Lucy clambered up the ladder and into the treehouse.

Benjamin and Natalie gave Lucy identical smiles, then brushed hair from their eyes with the same quick gesture. They looked exactly like brother and sister. They looked like their parents, too. Nothing out of the ordinary here.

"What are you staring at?" Benjamin asked.

"Nothing." Lucy sat down, tried to look casual. "I want to ask you guys something that's obvious, that I wouldn't bother asking, except I have an assignment. You're part of a pretty typical American family, right?"

In the silence that followed her question, Lucy knew what the answer was, though she didn't know why.

"Go ahead," she said glumly. "Tell me why you're not typical."

"You know the song I was just singing," Natalie said. "Well, what do you think it's about?"

Lucy shrugged.

"It's about being Jewish," Benjamin said.

"Being Jewish is not being typical," Natalie said. "At least, not in this neighbor-hood."

"Oh," Lucy said. Benjamin was always talking about his bar mitzvah, Lucy remembered. He was spending a lot of time studying for it.

"You should understand, Lucy." Natalie strummed a chord. "You're different, too." Natalie and Benjamin smiled their identical smiles at Lucy.

Lucy stood unsteadily. "I don't want to be different." She couldn't think very clearly. She felt tired.

"Why?" Natalie asked.

"Because," Lucy said. The word came out soft and unsure, more like a question than an answer.

"You're awfully quiet," Dad said that night at dinner.

"Aren't you hungry?" Mom asked.

Lucy slumped lower in her chair. "Not really. There are some holes in my case."

Mom went to the kitchen counter and came back with the Priority Mail envelope. "We were going to show you this on Saturday, but maybe now is a good time. In case you want to get to work." Mom pulled some papers from the envelope. "When this family tree thing came up, I called the adoption agency we worked with, when we adopted you."

"Parents need advice too, Lucy," Dad said.

Lucy took a gulp of milk.

"The agency sent us examples of how other adoptive families have worked with this assignment," Mom said. "I called some of our friends, too, to see if they had dealt with it."

Lucy almost choked on the milk. "Who did you call?"

"The Petersons, the Schneiders, and the Moores."

Friends who were also adoptive families. Lucy wondered if these people were talking about her—about her dilemma. Maybe they thought *she* was the dilemma.

"Are those all you told?" Lucy's voice was hoarse. They knew other adoptive families, too.

Mom rested her hand gently on Lucy's arm. "Those are all I told."

"It wasn't yours to tell," Lucy said hotly.

"We're sorry." Dad rubbed the back of his neck; that's what he did when he felt worried. "We were trying to help."

"May I be excused?" Lucy was already standing.

Lucy shut the door to her room and threw herself on the bed. Now people knew that being different bothered her. Why did her mother have to talk about it with other people? Lucy pounded the pillow, then pressed her face into it and cried until she couldn't anymore.

She sat up then, and looked into the mirror above her dresser. There was her face, more red than brown from crying, and her black hair, plastered against her forehead and wet cheeks. There were her full lips—Rubber Lips, a mean kid had called her once, but Mom thought they looked beautiful, like cherries.

Lucy wondered if her birth mother had lips like cherries.

Lucy's mouth was trembling now. But she tried to smile; sometimes trying to smile makes you feel like really smiling, Dad always said.

Lucy did it—she managed a slight smile, and in doing so, caught a glimpse of her white teeth. The dentist said Lucy's teeth were so straight and strong, she probably wouldn't have to have braces. Perfect teeth, he'd called them. The kind everyone wishes he or she could have. Thinking that made Lucy really smile, and then she laughed, because she looked funny—happy and unhappy at the same time. She'd never thought it was possible to be that way.

On her desk, hidden beneath her school books, was her list. Lucy had drawn lines through the names *Lucinda, Robert, Benjamin.* They all felt different, too. But there were still her parents' friends on her list.

The next morning Lucy watched Marco playing soccer. He was good—fast and aggressive, not afraid to fall down or get kicked in the shins. Marco's brother was a professional soccer player in Mexico. "My brother is famous in Mexico," Marco was always saying. "He teaches me moves all the time."

As if his brother lived only a few towns away, like the Keatons, the next name on Lucy's list.

Lucy closed her eyes and Marco disappeared. She tried to imagine visiting the Keatons, the better to study their case. She imagined ringing their doorbell. Then she imagined Mr. Keaton at the door, and opened her eyes.

Oh, no! Mr. Keaton was Mrs. Keaton's second husband. Their children, Dora and Seth, were children from Mrs. Keaton's first marriage. Mr. Keaton was a parent by marriage.

Maybe "adopted" sounded to Marco the way "stepfather" sounded to Lucy. Different. Maybe like something second best. But Mr. Keaton was always cheering for Dora at her ice-skating competitions; he was Seth's biggest fan at his piano recitals. Mr. Keaton couldn't be a better dad. He wasn't second best at all.

So the Keatons were different, too. Lucy was going to lose the bet with her parents. Even if the next two families were the same, she needed a total of three to make her case.

Marco scored a goal.

Lucy couldn't give up what she'd started, so she tried to think about the Smiths, the next family on her list. Mr. and Mrs. Smith had been married only once, for many years, to each other. Like Mr. and Mrs. Smith, the Smith kids were blond and blue-eyed. The oldest son, Brian, was already married to a blond and blue-eyed woman. Then there was Katy Smith, who was in college, and then the Surprise Baby—at least that's what the Smiths called Peter, though he was in eighth grade now. Peter was teaching himself magic. He loved to surprise people, which considering his history, was no surprise at all.

No, there was nothing surprising in this family. They were all the same. Typical. Exhibit A.

Maybe the Malones were Exhibit B. The Malones were more like family than

friends, and seemed a lot like the Smiths. But then Lucy remembered that they didn't always look happy, the way so many all-American families did on TV. Three years ago, Jack and Mary Malone's youngest child, Susan, was hit by a car and killed. Since then, Lucy had often heard Jack and Mary talking in low voices with Mom and Dad. Sometimes Jack and Mary sat in silence. Sometimes they cried.

Lucy sighed. You could look like everyone else and be like everyone else, and still have things hidden deep down, things most people never saw.

Lucy sat up so fast, she almost tipped back in her chair. She had an idea. It wasn't winning the bet the way she'd expected, but she wasn't so sure now she wanted to win that way anymore.

On Saturday morning, in the middle of raking leaves, Lucy announced, "It appears we only know families who are different."

"We know families we like," Mom said. "Those families happen to be different."

"And if a family did turn out to be the same, and every other family was different," Dad said, "then the family that was the same would be different."

Dad was using the kind of logic Lucy had been using since yesterday. The kind of logic that tipped the world upside down.

"Maybe." Lucy grinned at Dad. "But I found four examples, not three, of families who are the same." She pulled a piece of paper from her pocket, waved it like a flag in the air. "So I guess I won the bet."

Mom took the paper and read aloud, "The Petersons, the Schneiders, the Moores, and us."

Dad nodded. "Adoptive families," he said, his smile widening.

"Yeah," Lucy said. Like Lucy, all the children were born in Mexico. "I figured our families are about as typical as any other family. By our logic, anyway." Lucy picked up a particularly beautiful leaf. She slipped it in her jacket pocket for safekeeping. "But I still *feel* different, even from those people on my list."

"Oh, Lucy," Mom said. "That's because you're Lucy." Then Mom held Lucy close.

"Now," Dad said, "let's find the best spot for that flower bed."

Lucy spun away in a circle, her arms wide open, taking in the yard.

"Someplace where they'll grow stronger and bigger and more beautiful every year," she said.

That evening Lucy began to make a family tree. It happened this way. Mom and Dad presented their idea to Lucy—the one from the Priority Mail envelope—a traditional tree with a branch for the birth family. And Lucy presented her idea to them, the one blooming in her mind. After some discussion, Lucy decided to combine both ideas and complete the assignment, her way.

Lucy made a Tree of Life. She softened green modeling clay, shaped it into branches, and molded the edges so that the tree was round, like the Tree of Life in her wooden chest. Then she took brown clay, mixed it with pink, and formed herself. She covered her figure with a clay reproduction of the Mexican shawl her parents had given her. Then she placed the figure at the center of the Tree. The little Lucy was stretching out her arms, as if ready to hug someone.

Now Lucy molded a miniature Mom and a miniature Dad, and placed them on the Tree. She made bright angels. And then she made her birth parents, the people she'd always imagined.

When she was finished, Mom said, "Oh, Lucy, you did it! They remind me of you."

Dad said, "They look like kind people."

Lucy couldn't say anything. She put her birth father next to her birth mother at the bottom of the Tree. Both of them were reaching up, so that their hands touched the soles of Lucy's shoes. It looked as if they were supporting her.

Now all Lucy had to make were the birds and fruits and flowers. Then the Tree was finished. She baked it in the oven to set the clay. With Mom's help, she pulled the Tree out. It was burning hot, but solid. There were no cracks that Lucy could see.

The next day, Dad drove Lucy to school. She kept twisting around to make sure
her Tree was safe in the back seat. That morning they had anchored the Tree to a large
breadboard, and in the process broken a branch. They'd glued the branch back on, and
it looked fine. But Lucy knew to handle her Tree with care.

Dad helped her carry it inside. The classroom was noisy, with kids rushing this way
and that, taping up family trees. Dad and Lucy found an empty spot, and together stood
Lucy's Tree of Life against the blackboard.

"It glows with color," Ms. Magritte said.

Lucy caught her breath. She hadn't realized Ms. Magritte was standing right there.

Last night, Dad had telephoned Ms. Magritte to remind her how difficult this assignment might be for some people. He suggested that in the future, she offer not just one example of a traditional family tree, but clearer options for different kinds of families. Lucy had given Dad permission to make the call. But now she edged her way into the corner, trying to make herself smaller.

"Thank you, Lucy," Ms. Magritte said.

"Thank you?"

Ms. Magritte smiled. "Thank you for creating something truly original. *Your* family tree."

Lucy stood tall. Dad grinned at that, kissed Lucy, and headed out the door.

Ms. Magritte let the class take ten minutes to look at the family trees. Lucy couldn't help but notice the large group clustered in front of hers. And Lucy couldn't help but notice something else, too. True to her new logic, many of the family trees had something unique about them.

There were even two other adopted kids—kids Lucy hadn't known were adopted. One of them, a boy named Sam, had made a tree similar to hers, only he'd drawn it on paper. Lucy wondered if Sam's parents had received a Priority Mail envelope, too. She would ask him later, when they were alone.

Lucy found herself standing in front of Marco's tree. She couldn't turn away, because Marco was walking toward her. "What do you think?" he said.

Lucy studied Marco's tree. She couldn't lie; she had to tell the truth.

"It's beautiful," Lucy said.

"Yours is, too," Marco said.

Lucy looked at Marco, surprised. But then she nodded. She knew that.

RETHINKING A FAMILY TREE PROJECT

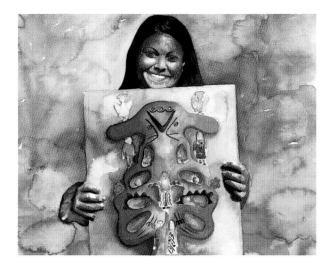

Families come in all shapes and sizes, since a family consists of a child and the people who love and care for him or her. When Lucy stopped to think about the families that she knew, she began to realize that there are lots of different kinds of families. She knew a family where the mom worked and the dad stayed at home, where there had been a divorce and a stepparent was part of the family, where two women were raising a child together, and other families with adopted children. If Lucy had kept looking, she would have found children at her school who were being raised by single parents, grandparents, or foster parents. Some might have lost a parent to death or incarceration or abandonment. Some might live in big houses, others in apartment buildings, and some might be living in a homeless shelter. Lucy would also have found children with different religions, different family customs, physical differences, different learning styles, and even different languages.

With so much diversity in our communities and schools, let's rethink some of our traditional school activities and assumptions about families so that we are inclusive, and no child feels denegrated, denied, or overlooked in any way. Many schools still have classroom activities based on holidays, family trees, autobiographies, baby pictures and family memorabilia, Mother's Day and Father's Day, and family background research or genetics. Offering children the option of participating and providing an alternative project will let each child approach the task at his or her own comfort level. Some children may wish to keep information about themselves and their families private, and they should be allowed to do so in a way that doesn't single them out. With a little creativity and foresight, we can make these activities a comfortable learning experience for more students—and contribute to each child's esteem at the same time. A new approach to the family tree project is a good start.

FOR YOUNGER CHILDREN

My Home: Children draw and name the people they live with inside a simple house frame.

The Loving Tree: Drawing a tree with heart-shaped fruit at the end of the branches, children draw themselves on the tree trunk and then draw the faces and names of people whom they love (and tell why) inside the hearts. A variation of this is the Caring Tree, where instead of filling in the hearts, at the end of the branches children draw the heads of the people they care about and briefly tell how each person cares for them.

A Tree with Roots: Children put themselves on the trunk, and then fill in the roots and branches with other family members. They could use the roots for birth parents or foster parents or birth siblings, and then use the branches for adoptive or stepparents, other parents, siblings, and other family members.

Family Houses: This approach uses family houses instead of a family tree, to show linkages between family members and to show how family members, such as parents, have moved from one home to start another with new members.

The Hedgerow: Children draw each current family member as one bush in a row of hedges. Roots can signify birth parents, grandparents, foster parents, different countries of origin, etc.

FOR OLDER CHILDREN

The Genogram: This diagram approach uses symbols to represent different genders (a square for males and a circle for females), with straight lines connecting parents to each other and to children. An X over a symbol indicates a death, and a diagonal line crossing a connecting line indicates a divorce. Households are enclosed within an elliptical circle around the figures that are part of a child's current family unit. This can be adapted to include important people in a child's life. A Line Diagram is a similar approach.

The Wheel Pedigree: This system of divided concentric circles or half circles places the child at the center, with parents in the next circle, grandparents in the next, etc. In a full circle, one side can be used for a birth family and the other side for the adoptive or foster family. Names, along with other information such as talents, interests, nationality, etc., can be added where known.

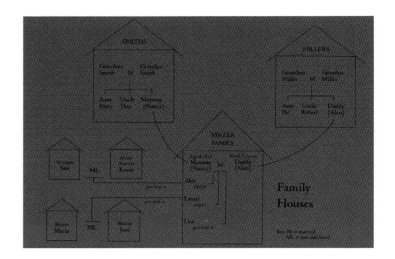

Family Houses

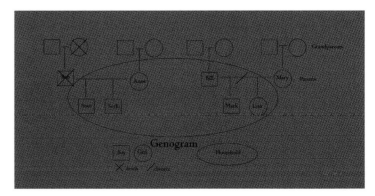

Genogram

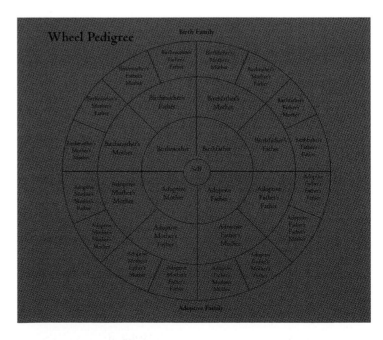

Wheel Pedigree

Tilbury House, Publishers
2 Mechanic Street
Gardiner, Maine 04345
800–582–1899   www.tilburyhouse.com

First Printing: May 2001
10 9 8 7 6 5 4 3 2 1

- For my daughter, my dear one, Magdalena. —KHS
- In loving memory of my Uncle Jim, and to family and friends who always believed in me. —SGG

Library of Congress Cataloging-in-Publication Data
Schreck, Karen Halvorsen, 1962–
    Lucy's family tree / Karen Halvorsen Schreck ; illustrated by Stephen Gassler III.
        p. cm
    Summary: Lucy, an adopted child from Mexico, is convinced that her family background is too complicated for
    her to make the family tree she is supposed to create for a homework assignment.
        ISBN 0-88448-225-1 (alk paper)
        [1. Identity--Fiction. 2. Adoption--Fiction. 3. Family--Fiction. 4. Genealogy--Fiction. 5. Schools--Fiction.
        6. Mexican Americans--Fiction.] I. Gassler, Stephen, ill. II. Title.
    PZ7.S37835 Lu 2001
    [Fic]--dc21   2001027213

Design by Geraldine Millham, Westport, Massachusetts • Color separations and film by Integrated Composition
Systems, Spokane, Washington • Printing and binding by Worzalla Publishing, Stevens Point, Wisconsin.

More Resources

Rethinking Schools   www.rethinkingschools.org
A nonprofit organization dedicated to the belief that classrooms can be places of hope, where students
and teachers gain glimpses of the kind of society we could live in, and where students learn the academic and
critical skills needed to make that vision a reality. Offers an online journal and many teaching resources.

Teaching Tolerance   www.splcenter.org
This extension of the Southern Poverty Law Center addresses classroom themes of tolerance, respect, and
community building, publishes the free *Teaching Tolerance* magazine, and provides many resources for teachers.

Adopting   www.adopting.com
Internet adoption resources, with hundreds of links and resources.

Family Diversity Projects   www.familydiv.org
This nonprofit is devoted to educating students, parents, teachers, politicians, religious leaders, communities,
and the general public about family diversity. It offers exhibits, reading lists, and web link recommendations.